Amish Christmas Dreams
Book 2
(The Christmas Miracle)

Rebekah Fisher

Copyright © 2018 by Rebekah Fisher. All rights reserved. Printed in the United States of America. No part of this book may be used or reproduced in any manner whatsoever without written permission except in the case of brief quotations embodied in critical articles or reviews. This book is a work of fiction. All names, characters, businesses, organizations, places, events and incidents are used fictitiously.

A NOTE FROM THE AUTHOR

I have always been fascinated by the simple Amish lifestyle and their deep faith and commitment to God.

As one who also loves God's Word and loves to impart hope and encouragement to others, my prayer is that you will find this book not only enjoyable to read, but find it inspirational and be reminded of God's everlasting love, care, and faithfulness.
May you blessed as you read these pages.

Much love,

Rebekah Fisher

To be updated with new book releases, be sure to join my newsletter.
Visit here: http://eepurl.com/boj6j

CONTENTS

A Note from the Author	i
Chapter 1	1
Chapter 2	6
Chapter 3	10
Chapter 4	15
Chapter 5	21
Chapter 6	29
Chapter 7	36
Chapter 8	45
Chapter 9	51
Chapter 10	58
Chapter 11	67
Thank You!	74
More Books by Rebekah	75

CHAPTER 1

The children's exuberant voices filled the single room of the schoolhouse as they practiced for the Christmas program. As the song came to an end, Katie Ebersole clapped, beaming in delight. She turned to Leora Miller, who sat in a chair beside her. "You've done such a *gut* job with the *kinner*. And my little *shveshtah is* so much more confident since she sang at the Christmas program last year."

"I'm so proud of her." Leora smiled. "Of course, Tyler has a lot to do with that, helping her learn some of the *Englisch* songs."

Katie laughed. "He always says he wishes he could have learned Pennsylvania Dutch as quickly and easily as Anna learned English. But she's also had a wonderful teacher, Leora. You do such *gut* work with the *kinner*."

"*Danke*." Leora smiled then turned to the children. "*Danke, kinner* you did well. You may have fifteen minutes' recess."

With a clamor of excitement, the children hurried out into the schoolyard to play, talking about their parts in the upcoming Christmas program. The older children helped the little ones to pull on their coats before ushering them outside. Despite the cold air and snow on the ground, the sun was shining, and Leora was glad to see them having fun. She breathed out a long sigh. "*Danke* for coming to help me with the *kinner* today. With Beth not able to help me today, I don't know how I'd get everything done."

"I'm happy to help." She smiled. "Christmas is always such a busy time of year with the *kinner*."

"*Jah*, so very busy. What are your plans for Christmas?" Leora asked.

"Well, Tyler and I will have dinner at my *daed's* house on Christmas Day. Tyler has been working hard on a new harness he's making for *Daed's* mare, and I'm cooking and baking fit to burst." Katie laughed. "But I'm so grateful to *Gott* that *Daed* was able to give Tyler some extra work in the shop so he could buy our new horse."

Leora nodded. "Tyler has adjusted so well to our Amish ways," she said, "but it must be hard. Most Amish men have decades to learn the skills that he's having to learn in a year."

"Exactly," Katie said. "It has been difficult at times, but always worth it." Love filled her smile. "I would move mountains for that man, and together with *Gott*, that's exactly what we're doing."

Leora put an arm around her best friend. "I'm so glad for you, Katie. You deserve to have found happiness."

Katie hugged her back, holding her tightly. "I know your turn is coming. You'll meet a man who's perfect for you and soon you'll have your own wedding and house and *kinner*."

Tears filled Leora's eyes. "I hope so," she said. "But I don't think..." She looked down, trying not to cry. "I don't think that's going to happen too soon. Not with everything the way it is at home."

"*Ach*, Leora, how is your *grossmammi?*"

"Not good." Leora frowned. "The cancer is eating away more of her brain every day. She's forgetful now too; some days she recognizes me, some days not. She's also nauseous and has headaches often. *Mamm* and I spend every extra moment we have caring for her."

"Is there nothing more the doctors can do?"

Leora shook her head. "Nothing. They say that it was discovered too late. It's too big to remove it, and her treatments most likely won't work on this type of cancer. All that is left is to..." She struggled to get the words out, tears running down her cheeks. "All that is left is to keep her comfortable in her last few months," she said, and began to weep.

Katie cuddled her close. "I'm so sorry, Leora. Your *grossmammi* has always been so kind and wise. It must be terrible to see her suffer."

"*Jah*, she suffers so much," cried Leora. "I try my best to make it easier for her, but still she has so much pain and it's hard on her when she can't remember simple things. She gets so frustrated."

"You're doing everything you possibly can, my friend," Katie said. "The rest is in *Gott's* hands. He has a plan, and He knows what He's doing even though it seems so confusing."

Leora wiped away her tears. "He could still heal her, even

now," she said. "He's a *Gott* of miracles. And I also know we must all go to be with Him when it's our time. But I don't understand why she must suffer so. I just wish she didn't have to go through all this." She covered her face with her hands. "I want my *grossmammi* back. It's just *Mamm* and I baking all the Christmas cookies; she can't help like she used to. She doesn't even remember that it's Christmas. It's like…" She gulped. "It's like we have already lost her."

"Don't say that, Leora." Katie kissed the top of her friend's head. "As you say, *Gott* can heal her yet. But we must leave it all in His hands and trust Him, no matter what happens. He knows the plan He has for her and He'll give you the strength you need, too."

Leora nodded. "*Jah*, He will. He already does." Leora smiled through her tears. "I just wish I understood His plan."

"I know." Katie sighed. "It's always hard to trust Him when we can't see what He's doing. But remember how worried I was when I first met Tyler? *Gott* had a plan even though I had little faith. I know He'll have something good come of this, in a way that you never saw coming."

Leora hugged her friend. "*Danke*, Katie. That's what I needed to hear. You're a wonderful friend."

"You are even better!" Katie hugged her back. "And remember, anytime you need any kind of help, just let me know. Tyler and I will do anything we can to help you. You know that."

"I know. *Danke*." Leora stood up, smoothing her dress. "Let's bring the *kinner* back inside and run through the program one more time." She grinned. "It'll be the best Christmas program yet!"

"*Jah*, indeed it will," Katie said, laughing.

CHAPTER 2

Elijah Hershberger could hear the soft hum of the dialysis machine as he hugged himself, shivering. By now he was used to the icy feeling in his veins, but it was still unpleasant.

A nurse hurried over to him. She had red curly hair and a name-tag that read "Rosie".

"Cold getting to you, Elijah?"

"A little," Elijah admitted, smiling at her. "As usual."

"We'll get that sorted right out for you." Rosie bent down, adjusting the heater in the dialysis chair. Elijah felt warmer at once. She grabbed a blanket from the cupboard and tucked it over him.

"Only twenty minutes left," she said. "You'll be out of here in no time. How's the nausea?"

"It's okay," Elijah said.

"Good. Let me know if it gets bad, then I can give you something for it."

"Thank you," Elijah said. "I appreciate your caring."

"It's my pleasure." Rosie gave him a little pat on the shoulder and bustled out of the room.

"You should be used to it by now." The man in the chair next to Elijah spoke in a joking tone. "It's not like this is your first dialysis treatment."

Elijah laughed, shifting uncomfortably in his chair. "I'm usually not as well prepared as you are, Lawrence."

Lawrence smiled. He was about Elijah's own age and had also been diagnosed with chronic kidney disease. They had been having dialysis treatments together for the past two months. His skinny body was bundled in layers of coats. "Hopefully we won't have to deal with these treatments for much longer, hey?"

Elijah sighed. "That would be something. You're on the transplant list too, aren't you?"

"Yeah." Lawrence shrugged, trying to smile. "Been on the list for three years. What about you?"

"Two years," Elijah said. "But hopefully soon we'll both get kidneys and be able to live normal lives."

"I hope so," Lawrence said. "I read something the other day that said that twenty-one people die every single day while waiting for a transplant." He sighed. "At least we only need kidneys, not hearts or lungs, and we can still get dialysis. But it's still sad that less than half of people in America are organ donors at all."

Elijah said nothing, looking down at his boots and wondering if this was his fate for the rest of his life—to have to make arrangements with a driver three times a week and sit for hours in this little room. He shifted in his chair, feeling an uncomfortable tug on the catheter that was implanted in his chest.

"I'm sorry," he said. "I have no idea if Amish people can be organ donors at all."

"They can," Elijah said. "It's an act of sacrifice and love that God approves of. My whole family signed up after I was diagnosed."

"But none of them are a match?"

Elijah shook his head. "My parents, three sisters and four brothers, and not one of them were a match."

Lawrence grimaced. "That's terrible luck."

Elijah shrugged. "If it's God's will, I'll get a kidney."

"Can your family afford a transplant?" Lawrence asked. "These medical bills must be draining… and they're farmers, right?" He frowned. "Do Amish have medical insurance?"

"No, we don't," Elijah said. "We depend on the community to come together for such things, and our community did just that. It only took a few months to raise the money I need for the transplant surgery. My parents work very hard to pay my medical bills, but the community also helps every month."

"That's amazing." Lawrence sat back in his chair. "I can't imagine my town doing that for me. It must be great to be Amish."

Elijah nodded. "I would never change, but sometimes I admit I envy the English at times, God forgive me."

"In what way?"

"Well, you have a job, don't you?"

"Yep, I do computer programming."

"A job where you can sit down all the time?"

"Yep."

Elijah spread his hands. "There's my problem. There's not much work that isn't physical for an Amish man. For me, I get tired so easily when I do physical work. I always have to stop to rest. Plus, I feel nauseous often." He hung his head. "I'm nothing but a burden on my family."

"Don't see it that way, Elijah." Lawrence paused for a moment. "Is that really how your family sees it?"

"Oh, no, they don't." Elijah said. "They believe that God has a plan for me and that He allowed this kidney disease for a reason. I don't see what it is, but I try to trust in Him as faithfully as they do. I just wish there was a way that I could help them more."

There were a few moments of silence. Elijah leaned his head back against the chair, feeling tired, as he always did, these days.

Lawrence spoke up in a brighter tone. "So, the Amish have Christmas too, right?"

Elijah appreciated his friend's efforts to cheer him up. He smiled, opening his eyes. "Oh yes, of course. The school children spend months preparing for a Christmas program where they sing, and give a Nativity play for their parents. We also have Christmas dinner every year–usually more than once so that we can get around to visiting all of our friends and family."

"That sounds nice," Lawrence said. "Do you eat turkey?"

"Once in a while, but we usually have roasted chicken or beef with potatoes and salads and lots of breads and pies. It's always a very hearty dinner."

"That sounds nice. My family also makes a hearty meal. But we usually always have turkey or ham." Lawrence continued with more curious questions. "And I'm guessing you don't decorate a Christmas tree?"

"No." Elijah shook his head. "No, that's an English tradition. We are focused on family and friends and the true meaning of Christmas, which is the birth of Jesus. We do put candles in the windows and wreaths on the door as a sign of welcome, though. We also send Christmas cards to our friends and put our own cards all over the house as a reminder of how well we are loved by our English and Amish friends."

"Duly noted." Lawrence grinned. "I won't send you a card with a Christmas tree on it, then."

Elijah chuckled. "My sisters are already working on a card for you."

"Speaking of kids, do you guys do the Santa Claus thing?"

"Of course not." Elijah shook his head violently. "Santa has no roots in the Bible, and it's inappropriate and unnecessary to tell the children such fairytales."

"So, they don't get presents?"

"Yes, they do get presents from their parents and family and friends. Usually helpful things, but we often give toys to the little ones. I've been helping my mother when I can to sew dolls for my little sisters and nieces." Elijah shrugged. "It's not something an Amish man would usually do, but I have to keep my hands busy somehow."

Lawrence grimaced. "I can't imagine having to go through life without a TV to watch, especially when you're exhausted."

"I read a lot. But yes." Elijah sighed. "The time can often go by slowly."

Just then, Rosie came back into the room, carrying a clipboard. "All still okay here, boys?"

"Doing okay," Elijah said.

Rosie laughed. "By now, you probably know better than I do how your dialysis is going."

She came over to Elijah and pushed his shirt aside, checking the flow of blood through the catheter.

She adjusted it slightly, which tugged at the catheter. Elijah flinched. "Sorry," Rosie said. "Is it painful there?"

"No, no," Elijah reassured her. "Not more than normal."

Looking a little worried, Rosie felt around the catheter site. "It's not hot. I'm just always careful of infection there. Have you been keeping it clean and dry?"

"Always," Elijah said.

"Of course, you have. You're a good patient, Elijah." Rosie laid a tender hand on his shoulder. "It can't be easy for you."

Elijah sighed, staring around the same old hospital room

where he had to sit for hours three times a week. "No," he said quietly. "It's not."

CHAPTER 3

Leora gazed at the children in her class who were bent busily over their work, making Christmas cards for their friends and families. She had helped them each to choose a design and now they were cutting shapes out of sheets of colored paper and sticking them onto their cards.

She went over to one of the wooden tables and helped Anna Ebersole to cut out a candle shape from a sheet of yellow paper. "There you go!" she said, as Anna lifted the shape carefully. "That's a perfect candle. *Gut* job, Anna."

"*Danke*." Anna grinned. "Katie and Tyler are going to love their Christmas card."

"*Jah*, I know they will." Leora kissed the top of Anna's *kapp*. "What are you going to write in it?"

"I think a Bible verse."

"That's a wonderful idea!"

Leora straightened up and walked towards her desk. She had barely reached her desk when suddenly the door swung open and hit the wall with a loud bang, making all the children jump. Her older brother, Nathaniel, came bustling in. She was about to chastise him for disrupting the class when she saw that his eyes were wide with fear. "Nathaniel, *bruder*, what's wrong? What happened?"

"It's *Grossmammi*," he gasped.

Leora put a hand over her mouth, feeling dizzy with shock. "What has happened?"

"She collapsed. She's going to the hospital in the ambulance." Nathaniel motioned towards the door. "You must come, Leora. Quickly."

Leora looked across at her assistant teacher, who waved a hand. "Go! I'll take care of the *kinner*."

"*Danke,* Beth!" Leora grabbed her coat and ran after Nathaniel, jumping in the buggy.

He cracked the reins, pushing the horse to go as fast as it could. Leora's heart hammered as she clung to the seat. *Gott*, she prayed. I know that *Grossmammi* must go home, eventually. But not today, *Gott*. Please, not yet.

❊

Elijah's dialysis treatment was almost done. He felt exhausted. He sat with his head leaning against his chair, trying to ignore the cramps in his lower legs and the rising nausea. He knew that dialysis was keeping him alive, but he also knew that as soon as he got home, he would fall on his bed and sleep. He always felt extremely tired after his dialysis treatments.

Elijah heard a commotion outside the room. Sitting up, he looked through the door window into the corridor. He was surprised to see two fellow Amish people walking down the corridor. While he had seen other Amish at the hospital before, they were few and far between. These two were walking hand in hand and looked so much like one another that they had to be a brother and sister; both had striking blue eyes and frizzy, flyaway brown hair. A large amount of the woman's hair had pulled out from under her *kapp*, but that wasn't what caught Elijah's eye. It was the look on her face. Her eyes were puffy and red, and tears covered her cheeks. She looked like her heart had just been ripped right out of her body.

Elijah sank back down into his chair. He wondered what tragedy had brought her here. He leaned his head back and prayed for her.

❄

Leora's grandmother looked so small and helpless in the hospital bed. Her wrinkled skin was pale; there was an oxygen tube over her lip and an IV line running into her hand. She had managed to open her eyes and smile when Leora had come in, but she was too weak to talk.

Leora sat at her bedside, holding her grandmother's limp hand. She wished she could hear *Grossmammi* tell her one more time that everything was going to be all right.

A nurse came in and read something from the clipboard above her grandmother's bed and adjusted the oxygen tube. She smiled at Leora. "I'm afraid I'll have to ask you to leave now, dear. Your grandma needs to rest."

Leora gave *Grossmammi's* hand a squeeze, then laid it back onto the sheets. "Alright," she said, sniffling.

The nurse took Leora's arm and led her out of the room. "Is

your family here, sweetie?"

"Yes, they are. I think they have just gone down the street for something to eat. They'll be back soon."

"All right." The friendly nurse, "Rosie", Leora read on her nametag, settled Leora down into a chair in the waiting room. "You can wait right here until they get back. Do you need anything? Coffee?"

Leora shook her head. Rosie gave her arm a little squeeze and then went back outside. She remembered her conversation with the doctors. As soon as she and Nathaniel had arrived in her grandmother's room, they had seen the grave looks on their parents' faces.

"What's happening?" Leora asked the doctor, clutching her mother's hand.

"I'm so sorry, dear." The doctor had shaken his head. "As we know, your grandmother's cancer is terminal. It seems now that it has taken a turn for the worse. The pressure in her skull is rising."

"Isn't there anything more you can do?" her mother had asked.

"I'm sorry. We can keep her comfortable, but I have to tell you that we're reaching the end-of-life phase of this cancer."

His words had been so gently spoken, but they pierced Leora's heart. Why now, *Gott*? Please, just give me *Grossmammi* back. Heal her, *Gott*. I know You can.

"Are you all right?"

Leora was surprised to hear a strange voice speaking in the Amish language. She looked up. A young man stood in front of her, dressed in a plain Amish suit; his hands were in his pants pockets, and he looked concerned. "I'm sorry for intruding," he said. "You look very sad. Is there anything I can do for you?"

"*Nee*, I... I'm all right." Leora straightened up, wiping away her tears and trying to smile.

"You don't look all right."

"Please, I'm fine," she said, wanting to be left alone with her thoughts.

The young man sat down beside her and reached for the coffee table and grabbed a tissue box, holding it out to her. The kind gesture touched Leora. She took a tissue and tried to blow her nose as gracefully as she could. "*Danke*. I'm sorry."

"*Nee*, don't apologize."

"It's my *grossmammi*." Leora sniffed, grabbing another tissue to wipe her eyes. "She has cancer."

"*Ach, nee*." He shook his head. "I'm so sorry to hear that."

Leora shrugged. "It must be *Gott's* will," she said, "but I don't understand how He can possibly mean for all of this suffering to happen."

The young man sighed. "I know that feeling."

"I know He has a purpose for all of this, but it's so hard to see." Leora was amazed at how easy it was to talk to this man. He seemed so understanding, and it felt as though what she was saying really mattered to him. He listened intently as she went on. "I try to be faithful, but sometimes it feels like He's taking so much away from me, and it's hard to trust, especially when I have spent all my life trying to please Him as best as I can.

"He has His reasons for the trials and testings we go through. Remember, the Bible says we will go through trials. And that doesn't mean it's any kind of punishment," the young man said. "No more than the forty days and nights in the desert were punishment for Jesus. He was being tested." He touched her arm lightly. "Gott's ways are higher than ours and we don't always understand. He loves us and has a *gut* plan for our lives, no matter what it looks like through our eyes."

Leora nodded. She tucked some of her chaotic hair back into her *kapp*, suddenly aware of how messy she looked. "You are very wise."

"I have had a lot of time to read the Bible." The young man smiled. "Your *grossmammi* must be very dear to you."

"She's wonderful." Leora face brightened. "She's been living with us ever since *grossdaadi* died when I was a baby. She was always singing and sewing. She sewed me my first school dress, and she taught me everything I know about needlework of every kind. She used to sit with me on her lap and tell me Bible stories while she sewed."

"She sounds like an amazing person."

"She is truly amazing." Leora sniffed. "I know *Gott* can still heal her, but I must trust in His plan and have more faith that He knows what is best."

The door to the waiting room opened, and an Amish man with two little boys stood in the doorway. Leora recognized the boys as Ruben and Joshua Hershberger, two of her students.

"Elijah!" called their father. "Our driver is waiting."

"Coming, *Daed*!" The young man quickly stood up and smiled at Leora.

"*Gott's* ways are higher than ours, but He loves your *grossmammi* very much, and He's keeping a watchful eye on her. He has a plan for her earthly life and her heavenly life," he said. "Remember what the Bible says—He takes all things and works them together for our good."

Leora stared after him as they left, hardly believing what she had just experienced. Had she just spoken to a real man–or had God sent her a Christmas angel?

CHAPTER 4

Elijah's mother, Hannah, worked quickly, mixing together ingredients for cookie dough while he and his siblings sat at the table eating breakfast. Elijah watched as she whisked the milk and eggs together, but he wasn't really paying attention. His mind was back in the hospital lobby, talking to the girl with the flyaway hair. She had been so sad, yet despite the fact that her grandmother was dying, he could see her devotion to God and it had touched his soul.

"Can we have some cookies after breakfast, *Mamm*?" asked Elijah's youngest sister, Bethany, who was five.

"*Nee, dochtah.*" Hannah smiled. "First, we'll roll out the dough and cut out the cookies. You can help me with that part, then we'll bake them later this morning. All of you can help to decorate them after school and we can give them to our friends when they're done."

"But can we have some, too?" asked nine-year-old Ruben.

Hannah laughed. "*Jah*, we can have some," she said. "Now tell me, are all of you ready to walk to school?"

"*Jahhh*," chorused the three who were of school age. There were seven of them in total; Elijah was the eldest, and his two brothers were also out of school. Ruben, Joshua and Joanna were in school, and Bethany was too young. The two older boys were already outside helping their father to milk the cows. Elijah knew he should be with them, but he had been so tired after dialysis yesterday that he'd only woken up when his younger siblings came in for breakfast after chores.

"Are you sure?" Hannah asked. "Do you have everything Leora asked you to bring?"

"*Jah*, we do," twelve-year-old Joshua said. "We're finishing our Christmas cards today."

"I'm making a pretty one for you, *Mamm*," Joanna said.

Hannah smiled at her. "*Danke, dochtah*."

"Do you like Leora, Elijah?" Ruben asked, turning to Elijah.

"What?" Elijah looked up from his toast. "I haven't ever met your teacher."

"*Jah*, you did," Ruben said. "I saw you with her."

Hannah looked at the boy curiously. "When did you see your brother with Leora, Ruben?"

"Yesterday. At the hospital," Ruben said. "When we went to pick Elijah up from dialysis."

"*Ach!*" Elijah's face brightened. "Was she the one I was sitting with?"

"*Jah*," Ruben said. "The one that was crying."

"Have you met her before?" Hannah asked him.

"*Nee*, I just saw her at the hospital yesterday. She seemed upset, so I tried to make some conversation and help her feel better."

"That's kind of you," she said.

Elijah sunk back into his seat, knowing what was on her mind. He knew that she worried about him, thinking he might never find a girl to marry, even if he was given a transplant someday. He was nineteen already and couldn't go to any of the social gatherings where young Amish came together, like the singings, or community events. He seldom spoke to any Amish outside of his own family. He was too embarrassed. He felt useless compared to the other strong young Amish men who could shoe horses and milk cows.

But Leora was different. She had poured out her heart to him, and he'd loved listening to everything she had to say. He choked down the last of his toast, struggling against the nausea that he always felt. He had to make some kind of plan to speak to her again.

❄

When school was out, Elijah was waiting for his siblings, standing alongside his father's buggy. He had been nervous about driving the buggy fifteen minutes up the road to the school, but he took it slow and had arrived without feeling terribly nauseous. He watched as the bell rang and the children all rushed out into the schoolyard.

Elijah's little siblings all came running straight up to him, shouting his name. He laughed as they hugged him. "Elijah! You came to pick us up!" Joanna cried.

"*Gut* afternoon, *shveshtah*!" Elijah kissed the top of her head. "Did you all have a *gut* day at school?"

"*Jah*, we did," Ruben said. "We practiced our Christmas program again."

"Will you come and watch it this time?" Joshua asked.

"I hope to," Elijah said, not wanting to make any promises.

"Why did you come to pick us up?" Ruben asked. "We can walk home."

"I..." Elijah looked over towards the schoolhouse just as Leora stepped out of the classroom. She was laughing at something one of the children had said, and he noticed how pretty her smile was. He swallowed, trying to gather his thoughts. "I wanted to surprise you," he said.

"*Danke!*" Joanna flung her arms around his waist and hugged him, then scrambled up into the buggy.

"Ruben, look after the horse and buggy for a minute, please. Joshua, go ahead and climb in the buggy and sit with your sister. I'll be right back."

He walked across the schoolyard, trying to look strong and confident. Leora was kneeling in front of one of the little girls, tying her *kapp*. She was smiling, but there were dark rings under her eyes.

Leora straightened up and the little girl ran off to her parents.

"*Gut* afternoon," he said.

Leora jumped, putting a hand on her heart. "*Ach*! It's you." She smiled. "I half believed I had imagined you yesterday."

"*Nee, nee.*" Elijah laughed. "I'm quite real."

"That's a relief," Leora said laughing.

"I never introduced myself yesterday." Elijah tipped his hat. "My name is Elijah Hershberger. I'm Ruben, Joshua and Joanna's *bruder*."

"I thought I saw Ruben and Joshua with your *daed* yesterday." Leora smiled. "Leora Miller", she said, holding out her hand. "I'm pleased to officially meet you."

Shaking her hand, he asked, "How is your *grossmammi*?"

Leora looked down, biting her lip. "There is no difference. She's still in and out of consciousness and she hardly knows who she is, even when she's awake." She looked up at him, tears in her eyes. "I fear she is coming to the end of her life."

"I'm so sorry." Elijah laid a hand on her shoulder. "Like you said yesterday, *Gott* can still heal her. It's up to us to wait and pray for her healing, but also for His will. He has the power for any kind of miracle, but we must also trust in His plan, Leora."

"I know." Leora took a shaky breath. "I know that. But I love my *grossmammi*. I trust *Gott* has a plan, but at the same time, I don't... I don't want to lose her." The tears spilled over, and Leora hid her face in her hands, weeping.

Elijah wanted to wrap his arms around her, but he stood there helplessly. The truth struck him hard. He hated seeing this sweet girl in pain, and he wanted to do something to make that pain go away. He had been attracted to her at once yesterday, but he knew that he couldn't allow these feelings to go any further, no matter how much he enjoyed her company. He knew that in only a few years, unless he was able to find a kidney donor, Elijah would be in the same position as Leora's grandmother was now. Dialysis wouldn't keep him alive forever, and the chance of getting a transplant in time was low.

It broke his heart, but he couldn't allow himself to hurt her in that way. He chided himself for even coming to see her and stepped back. "I'm sorry to hear about your *grossmammi* ," he said gruffly. "I'll continue to pray for her. And for you."

She looked up at him with surprise on her face and nodded. "*Danke.*"

"I have to get back with the *kinner*. I'm sorry." Elijah hated the fact that his words had already made her look hurt. He turned and walked quickly back to the buggy.

CHAPTER 5

The children in Leora's class had finished their Christmas cards and were so excited to show their cards to their parents. When the bell rang, they rushed out into the schoolyard waving their cards. She followed them out into the schoolyard, smiling as some children ran up to their parents' buggies and others hurried off home. They were all talking excitedly, and their parents looked pleased.

"Katie!" Anna ran past Leora, hurrying up to Katie. "Katie, I made some cards and one is for you and Tyler!" Anna shouted.

Katie laughed. "Did you now?" She took the card Anna gave her and gasped. "It's so pretty, Anna. I love the colors you used and the candles you made along the edges. *Danke*."

"Anna made those all by herself," Leora said, reaching the buggy.

"They're beautiful!" Katie hugged her little sister. "Jump in the buggy and we'll quickly show them to Tyler."

Anna clambered into the back of the buggy. Seeing Leora standing there, Katie patted the driver's seat beside her. "You look like you have something on your mind. Let me give you a ride home–this new horse of Tyler's has so much energy, it will do him good to use some."

"*Danke*, that would be great." Leora climbed up beside Katie and they drove off down the lane. The horse's hooves crunched in the new fallen snow that had covered the landscape in a layer of white.

Leora listened to it trotting along for a few minutes before speaking. "Elijah Hershberger came to see me at school yesterday. Do you know him?"

"Elijah Hershberger." Katie frowned. "I don't think I know him."

"*Nee*, neither did I. Three of the Hershberger *kinner* are in my class, though."

"Why did he come to see you?"

"Well, I actually first met him the day before yesterday," Leora explained. "I was at the hospital to see my *grossmammi*, and he saw me crying in the waiting room." Leora blushed. "He came up and spoke to me, and he was so kind and compassionate."

Katie was smiling. "That was kind of him."

"*Jah*, it was. I was so happy to see him at school yesterday." Leora paused. "He's like the kind of man I'd like to get to know better."

"Then why do you seem unhappy?"

"Well, he acted a little strange yesterday. At first, he was just like he had been at the hospital–kind and encouraging. But then he suddenly just... sounded a little gruff and then he left in a hurry." Leora frowned. "I don't know what I did or said wrong."

"I don't think you did anything wrong." Katie shrugged. "Maybe something else was worrying him. He was at the hospital, after all. Do you know why?"

Leora suddenly felt ashamed and looked down at her boots. "*Nee*," she admitted. "I have no idea why he was there. I... didn't ask."

"Perhaps one of his family members is sick, too," Katie said. "You know better than anyone how stressful that is."

"*Jah*. I don't know why I didn't ask him, when he had been so caring to me," Leora said. She sighed. "He must think I'm quite selfish."

"*Nee*, not necessarily." Katie gave her an encouraging smile. "Maybe you should stop over at the Hershbergers' house and see him. I'm sure everything will be much clearer then."

"*Danke*, Katie." Leora leaned over and hugged her friend. "That's a great idea. I'll do that as soon as I get home."

※

Leora's father had explained to her where the Hershberger house was. She quickly grabbed some cinnamon friendship bread before hitching up the buggy and heading out. The drive was short, only about fifteen minutes, and there was still good daylight when she arrived at the house. It was a big house, and there was a group of black-and-white dairy cows standing beside the barn.

Elijah would probably be helping his father and brothers milk the cows. Leora stopped the buggy, tied up the horse and walked up to the front door, hoping that she'd get a chance to speak to him. She knocked on the door.

To Leora's surprise, Elijah answered it. "Leora!" he said, surprised. He looked pale and tired. "How are you?"

"*Gut, danke*." Leora glanced at the barn, wondering what Elijah was doing inside with his mother and the small children. "I came to apologize to you." She held up the bread, which was still warm and wrapped in a dishtowel. "And I brought some cinnamon bread for your family."

Elijah stared at her. "Apologize for what?"

"For yesterday." Leora frowned. "I... I realize now that I never asked you why you were at the hospital. You have been so kind and *gut* to me, but I've been selfish. I'm sorry."

"*Nee*, Leora, don't worry about it." Elijah smiled, taking the bread. "I didn't even think anything of it."

"I hope your family is well," Leora said.

"They are all very well. We're fine." Elijah stepped back, opening the door. "Come inside."

"My *mamm* has coffee on the stove, and she just baked some cherry pie."

Leora hesitated, but she found herself wanting to spend more time with him. "*Danke*," she said. "That sounds wonderful."

She stomped the snow from her boots and came inside. Following him into the kitchen, the smell of freshly baked pie wafted through the air. Candles lined the windowsills and a string of Christmas cards hung in the corners. Leora recognized Ruben, Joshua and Joanna's cards.

Elijah saw her looking at the cards. "The *kinner's* cards are very nice," he said. "They told me all about how much you helped them."

"They had a wonderful time making them."

An older woman came bustling in, holding some folded dishtowels. She paused when she saw Leora and smiled. Leora recognized her as her students' mother. "*Gut* afternoon," Leora said.

"*Gut* afternoon, Leora. I'm Hannah." Hannah's smile widened. "It's nice of you to stop by. Are my *kinner* doing all right in school?"

"*Ach, jah, jah.* They're doing well. No problems at all with any of them. They're wonderful *kinner.* I stopped by to talk to Elijah."

"Leora brought us some cinnamon bread, too," Elijah said, putting it carefully in the bread-bin.

"Is your pie ready, *Mamm*?"

"It certainly is. Please, have a seat." Hannah pulled out a chair for Leora. "Would you like some coffee?"

"*Jah*, I'd love some. *Danke.*

Leora sat down opposite Elijah. He smiled at her as Hannah brought them both plates of cherry pie.

"*Danke*," Leora said. She took a forkful of the pie, which was perfectly made. She savored the cherry filling, and the crunchy, buttery crust melted on her tongue. "This is delicious, Hannah."

"She makes the best cherry pie in Pennsylvania," Elijah said with a grin, but he only took a small bite of his pie and then laid his fork down.

Hannah laughed. "I'm glad you think so", she said, patting his shoulder. She poured them both some coffee. "Are you getting me new pie dishes for Christmas, son?"

Elijah smiled. "It's a secret."

"Elijah is always *gut* with gifts," Hannah told Leora. "This year he's spent hours helping me make gifts for his *shveshtahs* and nieces. He's learning to do some wood carving too."

Leora laughed. "My friend's husband, Tyler was trying to make some wooden toys for my little *shveshtah*, but he still has so much to learn about woodworking. He loves it though. But I think he gave up on them for this Christmas and bought her a book instead."

"*Jah*, I know who Tyler is. I'll admit, I wasn't sure he would adjust when Bishop Yoder first baptized him," Hannah said. "But he has surprised us all. He's one of us now."

Leora nodded. "His whole life was just a long *Rumspringa*, Katie and I say," Leora said. "He's Amish at heart. I bought him woodworking and farming books for Christmas. I think he'll learn the skills quickly."

Elijah looked over at Leora. "That's very kind and thoughtful of you."

Leora loved the expression on Elijah's face; it was sincere and gentle. "Tyler and Katie have been so *gut* to me. It's the least I can do for them."

They chatted for a while, and Leora found herself enjoying

Elijah's company so much, she didn't want to leave. They talked about children, animals, church, Christmas, and anything else that came to mind. It felt so easy to have a conversation with him.

They were still talking when the front door opened, letting in a gust of cold wind. Elijah's father came in, brushing the snow from his shoulders. "The milking is all done," he said. "Just in time, too. It's nearly dark."

Leora looked out of the window and saw that it was already dusk. "*Ach nee!*" She jumped to her feet. "I'm so sorry, but I better leave for home before it's too dark."

"*Jah*, I think that's a *gut* idea." Elijah stood up slowly. "I'll walk you to your buggy."

He held the door for Leora and they walked down the path together to where Leora's horse stood patiently waiting with his blanket draped over him. Elijah pulled the blanket off for her and helped her stow it in the buggy. "Will you be all right to drive home alone?"

"It's not far," Leora said. "I'll be fine, *danke*."

"Alright." Elijah looked up at her as she got into the driver's seat. "Be safe, now."

Leora was half hoping he'd invite her to come again soon, but instead he just stepped back, shivering, and pushed his hands into his pockets. She waved at him and then snapped the reins, heading down the driveway and onto the road. She felt as though she might just float away. Despite all her worries, Elijah had made her feel comfortable and happy for a while.

She hoped that she'd see him again very soon.

CHAPTER 6

Leora wiped a hand across her forehead as she finished mixing together the sugar, flour and shortening to make crumbs for the shoofly pie she was baking. "How many of these are we making, Katie?"

Katie was busy stirring a pot on the stove. "Four," she replied. "My family loves my *grossmammi*'s shoofly pie recipe–no matter how much I make, it never seems to be enough."

"It sure is a wonderful pie," agreed Leora quietly.

Katie put down her spoon, wiped her hands on her apron, and turned to her friend. "How is your own *grossmammi*?"

"She's... holding on." Leora didn't look up as she poured a molasses mixture over the first layer of crumbs in the pie dish. "Not really better, not really worse. But the doctors keep saying the same thing. It's only a matter of time...." Tears filled her eyes. "She has had a few moments when she knows who we are and where she is, and she seems very peaceful. But my poor *mamm* and *daed* are exhausted. And I... I just wish she could get better."

"*Ach,* Leora, I know." Katie came over and wrapped her arm around Leora. "Nothing I can say or do will make it easy, but I promise I'm praying for her and for you every day."

"That means the world to me." Leora said, managing a smile.

"Let's talk about something else." Katie helped Leora to add another layer of crumbs to the pie dish. "How did your talk with Elijah go yesterday?"

Leora found herself smiling without meaning to. "*Ach*, it was wonderful!"

"That *gut*?" Katie laughed. "What did he say?"

"He wasn't angry at all. He invited me in and his *mamm* gave us some coffee and pie and we had such a nice visit." Leora shrugged. "He's so kind, Katie."

Katie grinned. "I'm glad it went so well. He seems like a *gut* man."

"I think he is," Leora agreed. "I enjoy his company and he's so easy to talk to. But there's one thing I found strange." She frowned. "His *daed* has a dairy farm, and all of Elijah's brothers and *daed* were outside milking the cows when I got there. But Elijah was in the house."

"So, he wasn't helping his family with the chores?"

"*Nee*. I don't understand why not; he seems such a good-hearted and helpful man."

"Maybe he had just come inside for something, and when he saw you, he wanted to visit with you," suggested Katie.

"*Jah*, perhaps. I just didn't understand it. His *mamm* didn't seem bothered with it though. So maybe he had a good reason."

"Did you ever find out why he was at the hospital?" Katie asked, while rolling out the dough for another pie dish.

"I tried," Leora said, "but he didn't seem to want to talk about it, so I didn't ask."

"Maybe..." Katie began, but she was interrupted by a knock on the door. "Coming!" she called, quickly straightening her *kapp* and hurrying to the door. Leora turned her attention to layering the crumbs and liquid in the pie dish. She was distracted when she recognized the voice in the hallway. It was Elijah's.

He stepped into the kitchen. "*Gut* morning, Leora," he said. "Your *mamm* said I would find you here."

"Elijah!" Leora tried to hide her smile. "It's *gut* to see you. Please have a seat."

"I just came over to give you something." Elijah reached into his pocket and handed Leora a Christmas card. "Ruben, Joshua, Joanna and Rebecca wanted to give this to you. They've been working on it at home for days."

"That's so kind of them!" Leora took the card and admired it. It was decorated with pinecone and candle cutouts. "It's lovely. *Danke* for bringing it."

"Would you like some coffee, Elijah?" Katie asked, putting the kettle on the stove. "My husband, Tyler, is working in the barn, but he'll come in for some, too."

Elijah smiled. "In that case, *danke*, I would like that."

"*Gut*. Let me just call Tyler in from the barn." Katie went outside, and Leora poured the coffee.

"How is your *grossmammi*?" asked Elijah.

"About the same, *danke*. And how are you?"

"*Ach*, I'm *gut*. It seems you and Katie are quite busy today."

"*Jah*, she's preparing for a big Christmas dinner at her *daed's* house."

Tyler came in, followed by Katie; he was covered in wood shavings and looked frustrated. "*Gut* morning," he said, holding out a hand to Elijah. "Tyler Bailey."

"Elijah Hershberger." Elijah shook Tyler's hand. "Pleased to meet you."

"The same." Tyler laughed. "I'm glad you came, because now I'll get some coffee."

"Tyler!" Katie shook her head. "I would have made you some, anyway."

"I know. I'm just…" Tyler frowned, putting an arm around his wife's shoulders. "What's the word for 'joking'?" he asked in English. "Sorry. I'm still learning."

"Your Pennsylvania Dutch is *gut*, Tyler," Elijah encouraged him.

"*Danke*." Tyler took a seat at the table, and Elijah joined him. "It hasn't been easy, but everyone has been so kind in helping me to learn."

"It could not have been easy to convert from an *Englisch* life to an Amish one," Elijah said.

"It wasn't always easy, but it was certainly worth it." Tyler's face lit up. "I'm so much closer to *Gott* now than I was when I was still *Englisch*. Just look at Christmas. The *Englisch* Christmas is so much about money and parties. While there are many *Englisch* who do remember the holiday is about *Gott,* there are also many who celebrate Christmas without ever thinking about Him and the birth of Jesus. But for the Amish, He is what Christmas is all about."

"*Jah*, we spend time with family and we celebrate His coming, yet we do it all the time with Him in mind," Elijah said.

Leora continued to work on the pies, feeling happy despite her circumstances. She loved how Elijah spoke; how respectful and kind he was and how his eyes sparkled when he laughed. The conversation filled the kitchen and as soon as the pies were in the oven, the women sat down for a break and joined in.

It had been a little over a half-hour and the pies were already baked and sitting on the kitchen counter, their sweet smell filling the whole room, when Tyler finally stood up. "*Danke* for the coffee, Katie," he said. "I better finish up with that buggy wheel, so we can take it to visit your family."

"How's it going with the wheel?" asked Katie.

Tyler looked unhappy. "Not *gut*. I just can't quite get it straight."

"I can help," Elijah said, getting up.

"*Ach*, would you?" asked Tyler. "I'm having so many problems with it."

The two men went out, and Katie smiled over at Leora. "See?" she said. "I told you to give him a chance and he would prove to be helpful and hardworking."

"*Jah*, you did." Leora smiled. "Come on. Let me help you clean up the kitchen."

"Let's clean the table and the stove, then I'll do the dishes and you can take the men another cup of coffee," Katie suggested. "It's so cold in that barn."

The sticky molasses was hard to scrub off the table, and it was almost an hour later before Leora made more coffee and headed out to the barn. Tyler and Elijah were standing in the doorway, and Tyler was smiling. "*Danke* for your help, Elijah. The wheel looks much better now, and if it happens again, I can fix it myself next time."

"It's my pleasure," Elijah said.

As Leora came close, she noticed that Elijah was sweating. She was glad she was bringing him something warm to drink. "I brought you two more coffee," she said.

"*Danke!*" Tyler took his cup. "Tell Katie that the wheel is as good as new."

Leora held out a cup to Elijah, but he shook his head. "*Nee, danke*. I'm sorry, but I should go."

"Come on," Tyler said, clapping Elijah on the shoulder. "Stay for a few minutes. You've earned a rest before you go back home."

"*Nee*, sorry. I wish I could, but I have to go." Elijah took a few steps backwards and nodded to Leora. "*Danke* for your hospitality."

"Are you all right, Elijah?" asked Leora. "You look pale."

"*Jah, jah*. I'm fine, don't worry about me." Elijah smiled, but his face looked gray. "I'll see you another time." Before Leora could say more, Elijah turned around and headed briskly towards his buggy.

She ran a few steps after him, touching his arm to stop him just before they reached the buggy. "Elijah, wait."

Elijah stopped and turned to face her. "*Jah*?"

"I... I want to ask you something."

Elijah looked into her eyes. "*Jah*?" he said gently.

Leora noticed vaguely that he was swaying slightly, but she had to ask him. "Was there another reason you came here today?" she asked. "The *kinner* could have given me their card at the Christmas program." She held her breath, waiting for his answer.

Elijah rested a hand on her shoulder. It was trembling as if with weakness. "Because... though I barely know you," he said softly, "I care about you and I want to get to know you better. I have feelings for you, Leora, he blurted out."

She stared at him, her heart wild with hope. Reaching up to touch his face, she whispered back, "Me too. I have feelings for you as well."

Elijah smiled, opening his mouth to speak, but before he could say anything, his head lolled forward, his eyes closing. Suddenly, his knees buckled, and he collapsed to the ground.

"Elijah!" Leora screamed.

Tyler heard her cry and came running. Elijah was lying in a heap on his side, his hat knocked off, and his eyes closed. Leora crouched beside him and touched his neck. "His pulse is so fast," she cried.

"I'm calling an ambulance." Tyler ran towards the little phone shanty outside the back of the barn where he and Katie kept a telephone for emergencies.

Leora knelt beside Elijah and put her hand on his shoulder. "Please," she sobbed. "Please, wake up."

But he didn't stir. He just lay there, his breathing labored, as Leora wept.

CHAPTER 7

When Elijah woke up, he was in a hospital room. The walls were white and cold, and his bed felt strange. He blinked and raised a hand to rub his eyes, but an IV line in his arm yanked him back.

"Shhh." It was his mother's voice. She ran a hand through his hair. "Don't try to move," Hannah said.

Elijah looked around. His whole family was crammed into the little room. "What happened? I was at the Baileys' house."

"You fainted, son." His father was on the other side of him, a hand resting on Elijah's shoulder. "Tyler called an ambulance for you."

"*Ach, nee.*" Elijah gritted his teeth. He felt nauseous and looked to the side. He saw that he was plugged in to a dialysis machine. "Was it my blood pressure again?" he asked, frightened.

"It was, but..." his father swallowed. "The doctors say that there's more to it than that."

"What do you mean?" asked Elijah.

The door to his room opened, and his smaller siblings shuffled out of the way so that a stern-looking man in a white coat could come inside. Elijah recognized him as Dr. Rivers, who had been treating him since he was diagnosed with chronic kidney disease when he was still in school. "Good afternoon, Elijah," Dr. Rivers said with a sad smile. "I'd hoped not to see you in this position so soon."

"Good afternoon," Elijah said slowly. "What happened to me?"

"Your blood pressure dropped, which caused you to faint," Dr. Rivers said, coming closer to Elijah and looking up at a screen above him that showed his vital signs. "But when you came in, we had to run some tests because of how low your pressure was." He sighed. "There's no easy way to say this."

Elijah swallowed, bracing himself. "Tell me the truth, Dr. Rivers." He prayed silently to God to give him strength.

Dr. Rivers put a hand on his shoulder. "Your condition has worsened. Your kidneys have lost what little function they once had, and your body is filling with toxins. Your dialysis treatments haven't been frequent enough to keep up." Dr. Rivers looked him in the eye. "You will need more frequent dialysis, and I'm afraid that unless you get a transplant soon..." He bit his lip. "The prognosis isn't good, Elijah."

Elijah felt his eyes fill with tears. "What does that mean? Am I dying?"

"Not yet," the doctor said. "But you could be soon, if you don't get a transplant. I'm so sorry, Elijah. We're doing everything we can for you."

Elijah tried to hold back the tears. "Thank you, Dr. Rivers. You have always done your best for me, and I appreciate your effort."

Dr. Rivers looked away, his voice a little rough. "I'll check back in with you in a bit," he said, and went outside.

"Let us pray," his father said. "*Gott* is still capable of a miracle." Elijah was shocked to see tears in his father's eyes as his family took hands. He lowered his head and prayed silently as his father led a prayer for healing. Afterward, Elijah prayed silently. *Gott, please be with my family. They have been so good to me even if I was a burden on them. If it's Your will, heal me. But whatever Your will, give me the strength to face it. Amen.*

Little Rebecca spoke up. "Is Elijah going to be all right?" she asked, her eyes filled with tears.

Elijah put an arm around his little sister and pulled her close. "*Gott*'s will is going to be done, *shveshtah*," he told her. He leaned his head back on the pillow, feeling exhausted. "Are Leora and the Baileys all right?" he asked his mother.

"They are shaken," Hannah said. "Leora is still here. She would like to speak to you if you feel up to it."

"*Jah*, please."

Elijah's family left the room, and Leora came in. Her eyes were red from crying, and she clutched her apron nervously in her hands. It still had a black molasses stain on it from the shoofly pie. "Elijah," she whispered.

"Leora." Elijah smiled. "*Danke* for your and Tyler's help in getting me to the hospital."

Leora nodded. "Are... are you all right?" Leora stared at the medical equipment around him, her eyes resting on the oxygen tube under his nose and the IV in his arm.

Elijah sighed. He knew it was time to tell Leora the truth. "*Nee*," he said gently. "I'm sick, Leora. I'm very, very sick." Tears ran down Leora's cheeks. They broke Elijah's heart. He struggled to sit a little more upright and held out an arm to her. "Come here." He took her hand as she sat down next to him.

"What's wrong with you?" she asked.

"I have chronic kidney disease," Elijah said. "I've been sick since I was twelve years old."

"So that's why you were here at the hospital the other day."

"*Jah*, that is why." Elijah sighed. "I have to have dialysis treatments several times a week because my kidneys can't clean my blood for me anymore. That's why I have this." He pulled down his hospital gown to show her the catheter implanted in his chest. "It's why I can't work on the farm with my family."

"Is this why you fainted this morning?"

"*Jah*." Elijah nodded. "I'm getting worse, Leora. My body has been living without kidneys that work for too long."

"Is there no cure?" Leora's eyes filled with tears again.

"*Jah*, there is a cure, and one that works very well." Elijah touched her shoulder. "But I might never be able to get it. I need a new kidney–a transplant from a living person or a donor that has recently died. But it's not easy to find a match, and I've been on a waiting list ever since I was first diagnosed. I might never get that transplant."

Leora grabbed his hand. "Then we must pray, Elijah. We must pray that *Gott* will give you a kidney."

"*Jah*, we must but you have to do something for me." Elijah put his hand over hers.

"Anything." Leora sniffed, wiping away her tears.

Elijah's heart ached at what he had to do, but he believed it was the best thing for her. "Leora... I need you to walk out of this room," he said as gently as he could, "and never come back."

Leora drew back. "What? Why? What have I done wrong?"

"Nothing!" Elijah shook his head, then gritted his teeth when the movement hurt. "Nothing," he said. "*Nee*, Leora, it's nothing like that. I wish..." He swallowed hard. "I wish I had never gotten sick, then you and I could be together. But it wasn't *Gott*'s will." He searched her eyes, hoping she would understand. "I can't do this to you. You've seen enough of hospitals and you've heard enough about death. The chance is that you would lose me, too."

"But I want to be with you, no matter what happens."

"I know you do, but this path may only lead to heartbreak, Leora. I'll likely not get a kidney in time, and even if I do, the transplant might not work." It took all of Elijah's strength to continue. "Please go," he whispered. "I can't see you hurt like this."

Leora's face was wet and shiny with tears. She stared at him for a few more moments, her eyes shining with pain, then she turned and walked out of the room. Only then did Elijah turn his face into the pillow and allow himself to cry.

CHAPTER 8

Wandering through the hospital's cold hallways with a broken heart, Leora made her way to her grandmother's room, hoping she'd be awake. When she walked inside, she thought *Grossmammi* was asleep at first. She looked so small and wrinkled on the big hospital bed, surrounded by machines and tubes. The room was filled with Amish Christmas cards; and at her mother's request, the English Christmas decorations that had been in the room had been taken down. Instead, a little Nativity scene stood on the bedside table along with *Grossmammi's* Bible.

Leora came inside and sat down on the chair next to the hospital bed. "*Grossmammi?*" she whispered.

Grossmammi turned her head and smiled. She looked strange without her *kapp,* her white hair lying loose on the pillow. "Leora," she said, reaching out to touch Leora's cheek. "My dear child."

Leora let out a sigh of gratitude. "I'm so glad you're awake," she said, taking her grandmother's bony hand.

"I feel quite wonderful, my love," *Grossmammi said*. "It's almost Christmas." She gazed around at the cards in her room, smiling.

"That's right, *Grossmammi*."

Grossmammi smiled. "I'm seventy years old, you know," she said. "Seventy years, yet every single day, I have been given a Christmas gift."

"What do you mean?" Leora asked, wondering if her grandmother was feeling confused again.

But her voice was clear. "My child, *Gott* gave us the greatest gift of all. One that we use in every second and with every breath." *Grossmammi* gave a contented sigh. "He gave us life, child. But not only life here, but eternal life." She turned to Leora, smiling, her blue eyes sparkling. "Isn't that the greatest miracle of all? Our *Gott* gave the gift of His own Son, and He gave His own life for us to have eternal life." She gazed up at the ceiling. "That miracle is what will bring me home."

Leora squeezed her hand. "You seem happy, *Grossmammi*."

"I am happy. I'm very excited." *Grossmammi* grinned like a little girl. "I'm going to have the most wonderful Christmas." Then she frowned. "But what's the matter? You've been crying."

Leora was desperate for *Grossmammi*'s wisdom. She searched for the right words. "Well I…"

"*Ach*, love." *Grossmammi* touched her cheek again. "Don't cry about me."

"*Nee*, I'm not–well, not right now." Leora wiped at her tears.

"What is it, then?"

"It's... it's Elijah Hershberger."

"Who is he?" *Grossmammi* put her head to one side. "Tell me everything, dear. I'm right here to listen."

"He's a young man I met here in the hospital when you were taken here a few days ago," Leora told her. "He is sweet and kind, and he has an amazing faith and trust in *Gott*."

Grossmammi beamed. "A man for you, Leora."

"*Jah*. Well, I hoped so. But this morning when he stopped by at Katie and Tyler's house, he fainted. They brought him to the hospital, and he told me..." Leora began to weep. "He told me that he's sick. He has a kidney disease and if he doesn't get a transplant, he's going to die."

"*Ach, nee.*" *Grossmammi* shook her head.

"I don't know what to do," cried Leora. "He says he wants me to stay away from him to save me the pain, but I want so much to know him better, *Grossmammi*."

"There is only one thing you can do." *Grossmammi* was starting to look tired again. She nestled her head back into her pillows. "Pray and seek *Gott*'s will, my child. He always knows best." Her eyes were closed now. "Keep praying for a miracle," she murmured. "I have a feeling there may be a donor for him right here in this hospital." She gave a little smile.

Leora let go of her hand and kissed her forehead. "*Danke, Grossmammi*," she said. "Sleep well."

"*Ach*, I will," *Grossmammi whispered*. "I will."

She drifted off to sleep, and Leora left the room. She thought of *Grossmammi*'s words about a donor being right in the hospital and a wild idea filled her mind. What if God had already provided a miracle, and *she* was that miracle? Elijah had said that a donor could be living or dead, which had to mean that one kidney was enough for a person to survive with.

Perhaps she could give him one of her kidneys. Excitement filled her heart. At that moment, she spotted the kind nurse who had helped her to the waiting room a few days ago—Rosie. She was walking past, pushing a tray with medical equipment on it.

"Rosie?" Leora called.

Rosie turned. "Oh, hello!" she said. "I was just going to stop by your grandmother's room."

"She just fell asleep," Leora said. "But I wanted to ask you something."

Rosie pushed the tray into a side room and closed the door, turning back to Leora. "Sure," she said. "What's on your mind?"

"A friend of mine is here in the hospital, too," Leora said. "He's got something wrong with his kidneys."

"Oh, are you talking about Elijah?" asked Rosie. Sorrow filled her eyes. "How can I help you?"

"I know he needs a new kidney," Leora said. "I wondered if perhaps... perhaps I could give him a kidney."

Rosie laid a hand on Leora's arm. "How old are you?"

"Twenty."

"Okay, good. There are some legal processes you'd have to go through, and you'd have to be sure. There are some risks to the surgery as well." Rosie smiled. "But let's not get ahead of ourselves. I guess you don't know if you're a match to Elijah or not?"

"No," Leora admitted. "I don't."

"Do you know your blood type?"

"No." Leora blushed. "Sorry."

"That's okay. Let's start with a blood and tissue type test before we do anything else," Rosie said. "You'll have the results by tomorrow morning, and all I need to do is take a little blood."

Leora had seen the doctors drawing blood from *Grossmammi* before. "Okay," she said.

"Come with me." Rosie smiled and took Leora's arm, leading her down the hallway and into a hospital room. Leora was a little nervous of the needle, but she was too excited to be scared as Rosie pushed the needle into her vein and filled a glass tube with blood. She was sure God would give her this miracle–she would be a match for Elijah. She just knew it.

"Great," Rosie said, smiling as she took out the needle and put a bandage on Leora's arm. "We'll know by tomorrow morning. Why don't you go home and get some rest?"

"Alright." Leora stood up, smoothing down her skirt. "I'll be here early."

Rosie squeezed her arm. "I hope I have good news for you then, honey."

Leora had to take a taxi to get home, but at least she had arranged that at the front desk before visiting *Grossmammi*. All the way home, she prayed desperately, begging God to make her a match for Elijah. *Please, Gott, bring us together. Please save his life with my kidney and let us be together.*

When the taxi dropped her off, she ran into the kitchen. Her mother was sitting at the table, writing Christmas cards to give to friends and relatives they planned to visit. "Leora, my *dochtah*!" She held out her arms. "Tyler came over and told me what happened with Elijah. I remember you telling me about him after he came to see you at the school. How is he?"

Leora hugged her mother. "He's very sick, *Mamm*," she said.

"*Ach, nee*. How so? What's the matter with him?"

"He has something wrong with his kidneys." Leora drew back, saddened to speak the words, but at the same time excited for the miracle she knew God could still give them.

Her mother frowned in concern. "Will he be all right?"

"We don't know." Leora sat down on one of the chairs at the kitchen table just as her father came into the room. "He needs a kidney transplant, or the doctors are worried that…" She took a deep breath. "That he won't live. He's been on a waiting list for a transplant for a long time, and he might not get a kidney in time."

"*Ach*, Leora." Her mother sat down beside her, taking her hand. "I'm so sorry."

"But there is hope, *Mamm*." Leora smiled. "I'm sure that *Gott* will give us a miracle." She knew her parents would be proud of her for wanting to help and give of herself to save another life. "Today I asked one of the nurses if they could test me to see if I would be a match for Elijah. If I am, then I want to donate one of my kidneys to him."

"What makes you so certain you'll be a match?" her father asked gently.

"Well, I'm sure *Gott* would want to give us this miracle," Leora said. "He can do this for us, and I'm sure He will."

Her father looked at her solemnly for a long moment before speaking. "I want you to spend some time praying on this matter. You cannot make a hasty decision about this and there could be risks to you."

"*Daed*, I would be helping to save another person's life. I am certain I want to do this."

"Then we will see how God leads."

Her mother hugged her closely. "We'll be praying with you, *dochtah*," she said.

❄

The next morning, Leora's father took her into town so she could arrange for a taxi ride to the hospital. She sat in the hospital waiting room wringing her hands nervously as she waited for Rosie to come out and see her. She and her parents had been praying for hours seeking His will, but she was certain that if she only trusted God and had faith in Him, He would give her a Christmas miracle. She looked at the little glittery angels that decorated the window and knew that real and powerful angels were surrounding her even in this moment.

Finally, Rosie came inside. Leora jumped off the chair, her heart beating quickly. "Am I?" she said, forgetting her manners in her excitement. "Am I a match?"

Rosie put an arm around her shoulders and they both sat back down on the chairs. There was sorrow in the nurse's eyes. "I'm so sorry, Leora." She paused. "Elijah's blood type is B positive, and you're an A negative."

Leora felt like she couldn't breathe. "What does that mean?"

"It means that if you gave Elijah your kidney, his body would see it as a foreign object, and it would reject the kidney." Rosie looked sad. "In other words, you aren't a match. You can't give Elijah a kidney."

"No, No!" Tears ran down Leora's cheeks. "I don't understand. Why didn't God make me a match?"

"I don't know, honey." Rosie hugged Leora tightly. "I'm so sorry."

CHAPTER 9

❄

Shaken to the core, Leora continued to sit in the waiting room for a long while, weeping. Her entire soul was screaming out to God. *Why didn't You provide a miracle, Gott? How are You going to save Elijah now?*

Wiping the tears from her eyes, she slowly stood to her feet and walked down the corridor still in a daze. She decided she'd stop by her grandmother's room before arranging for a taxi. Looking down, she turned the corner and almost bumped into Rosie, who was wheeling Elijah back into his room after having more bloodwork done.

"*Ach! Elijah!*" she said, startled.

"Leora, what's wrong? You've been crying. Is it your *grossmammi*?"

Leora followed Rosie and Elijah into his room. "I'll let you speak to Elijah alone, dear, once I get him settled back into bed." Rosie gave Leora's shoulder a squeeze.

After Rosie left the room, Leora sat down on his bed. Putting his hand on her shoulder, he asked, "What's the matter?"

"I thought I could be a donor for you." Leora said, sniffling. "I… I thought *Gott* would provide a miracle. But I had my blood tested, and it's not a match with yours. I wanted to give you my kidney, Elijah." She wiped the tears coming down her cheeks.

"*Ach*, Leora." Elijah hugged her. "You really wanted to donate your kidney to me?"

"*Jah*. I'm so sorry I couldn't."

"There's no need to be sorry. I'm honored that you would think of getting tested in the first place." Elijah drew her close to him. "*Danke*, Leora. That was very kind of you."

"I just wish I could have helped you."

Elijah's smile was gentle. "My life lies in *Gott*'s hands, not yours. But there's still much that you can do to help me."

"What can I do?"

"You can pray." Elijah squeezed her hand. "You can pray for me. *Gott* is still able to do a miracle, no matter what the circumstances look like. You know that."

"I know." Leora tried to dry her tears. "I was just hoping…"

"We have to trust Him, Leora."

"We have to surrender to Him." The voice in the doorway was Katie's. Leora turned to see her friend coming into the room. "I'm sorry, to interrupt, and I'll be very quick, but your *mamm* told me I'd find you here," Katie said to Leora. "I know you've been through so much this week, and I wanted to ask if you'd like me to help out at the Christmas program tonight."

Leora nodded and wiped her eyes. "*Jah,* would you? *Danke,* Katie."

Seeing that Leora had been crying, Katie sat beside her friend and wrapped her arms around her. "Leora, what's wrong?" she asked. "Is it your *grossmammi?*"

"It's me." Elijah hung his head. "I have a kidney disease, Katie. If I don't get a transplant soon, I'll not make it."

Katie's eyes widened, but she kept her emotions under control for Leora's sake. "*Ach,* Elijah. I'm so sorry to hear that."

"I was hoping that I could donate one of my kidneys to him," Leora told her. "But my blood type doesn't match his."

Katie hugged her tightly. "All we can do is pray and surrender to *Gott*'s will. He knows exactly what is best for us. Remember when I wanted to push Tyler away because he was *Englisch* instead of allowing *Gott*'s plan to unfold? It was only once I surrendered to *Gott* could He move powerfully in my life. And look at us now." Katie smiled. "It was you who told me to stay open to *Gott*'s plan. Now it's your turn."

Leora nodded. "*Danke.*" She looked at Elijah. "We have to hold on to Him."

Elijah extended his hands towards the girls. "Let us pray together," he said, and led them in prayer. "Dear *Gott,* please forgive me for pushing Leora away. I ask that You would come into our lives and let Your plan unfold. If it's Your will, please heal both Leora's *grossmammi* and me. We trust in Your plan *Gott,* no matter what that might look like. Amen."

Leora lifted her head. Suddenly, from outside, there was the sound of running feet and loud voices. Somewhere in the hospital, alarms were beeping. Leora was scared. She jumped to her feet and ran out into the hallway. With dread, she saw that the doctors and nurses were running in the direction of her grandmother's room.

"*Nee!*" she cried. "*Grossmammi!*" Her heart felt like it was standing still.

"Leora!" Katie called, but Leora was already running along the hallway. When she reached her grandmother's room, it was packed with doctors and nurses. But none of them were doing anything. They stood around *Grossmammi*'s bed as the heart monitor above her head showed a flat line. *Grossmammi* was lying very still, her eyes closed, and a small smile on her lips.

"Do something!" Leora cried out. "Why aren't you doing anything?" She rushed towards her grandmother, but Rosie grabbed her, holding her back. "Shhh," Rosie tried to soothe her. "Leora, honey. Your grandmother has passed."

"*Nee!*" Leora cried. "Please, save her. Please, do something! Can't you do anything?"

"I'm sorry, love." Rosie held Leora tightly. "There's nothing we can do. Your grandma has a DNR order—that means we won't do CPR on her. She didn't want us to try to resuscitate her." Rosie's voice was gentle. "She's gone to be with the God she loves."

The mention of God calmed Leora. She stared at her grandmother, her heart breaking, but at the same time knowing in her soul that *Grossmammi* was Home at last.

"Leora?" Katie came into the room. She looked at

Grossmammi and held out her arms to Leora.

Leora fell into Katie's arms and allowed herself to cry.

※

Leora sat in the waiting room again, staring at the enormous Christmas tree at its center. She sipped on a cup of juice that Katie had brought her. She had stopped crying even though she still felt numb with grief.

"I'm going to miss *Grossmammi* so much," she said brokenly.

"I know," Katie said. "But at least her suffering is over now, Leora."

Leora nodded. "And she is with *Gott* now. She told me yesterday she would have the best Christmas ever."

"She'll have a wonderful Christmas." Katie hugged her.

"*Jah*, she sure will." Leora wiped her eyes and smiled.

"Leora... don't you worry about having to run the Christmas program tonight. Beth and I can take care of it. I've already helped the *kinner* practice, so between the two of us it will work out just fine. If you'd rather stay home and rest, that's fine."

"*Nee, Nee*. I'll be fine. I've been looking forward to it for so long. I couldn't bear to miss it. *Danke* though, Katie."

Katie took her hand. "Then I'll be there to support you in any way I can."

Rosie came in, carrying a clipboard. Her smile was cautious, but her eyes looked excited. She sat down beside Leora. "How are you doing, honey?"

"I'm okay," Leora responded.

Rosie bit her lip. "Leora, there's something I have to tell you."

"Yes?"

"Come with me." Rosie stood up and held out a hand to Leora.

"I'll wait for you and take you home, Leora," Katie said.

"*Danke*, Katie," she said as she took the kind nurse's hand and allowed herself to be led to Elijah's room. He was awake, but he looked exhausted; there were dark circles under his eyes and he was very pale. "I'm sorry about your *grossmammi*, Leora," he told her.

"*Danke*," Leora said.

Rosie sat down on the bed beside Elijah and patted the space next to her. "Please sit," she said.

Leora obeyed and looked at Rosie.

"When your grandmother was first diagnosed with cancer," Rosie began, "she knew that it was terminal, and that the tumor would eventually kill her. And while she told me that she believed God could still save her, she also wanted to find a way to serve people, even in death."

Hope jumped inside Leora's heart. "Yes?"

"Well, your grandma signed up to become an organ donor. That means that when she dies, her organs can be taken out and given to somebody who needs them."

Elijah sat up. "What are you saying, Rosie?"

THE CHRISTMAS MIRACLE

Rosie took Elijah's hand and gave him a gentle smile. "I spoke to Leora's grandmother this morning," Rosie said. "And she said to me that she'd heard there was a young man named Elijah Hershberger in the hospital who needed a kidney. She told me that she wanted her kidney to be donated to you." There were tears of joy in Rosie's eyes. "She's a match, Elijah. She's a match for you."

Elijah's eyes were wide. "But she was so sick. How can her organs still be working well?"

"Her cancer didn't spread to her organs," Rosie said. "She died because of the pressure building up in her skull, not because of organ failure. And, because the cancer was terminal, she did not want chemotherapy or radiation. Her kidneys are still healthy."

Elijah stared at her. "So, you mean I can get a transplant?"

"You *are* getting a transplant, Elijah." Rosie grabbed his hand. "You're getting a transplant today. In fact, the doctors will be coming in to start your anesthesia in the next few minutes."

This time, tears of joy were running down Leora's cheeks. "Elijah!" she said. "It was all part of *Gott's* plan. He knew what He was doing all along. He let *Grossmammi* pass on today because He knew you needed her kidney. He's going to save your life."

There were tears in Elijah's eyes. "I can hardly believe it," he whispered. "Your *grossmammi* just gave me the best Christmas present I could ever have." He was crying. "She gave my life a second chance."

Leora put her arms around him, and they cried together. She felt that her heart had swollen so much with both grief and gratitude it might explode. *Grossmammi* was safely in heaven with the God she loved, and Elijah was going to get another chance at life. "*Gott*," she whispered a prayer. "You are so *gut* to us. You are so *gut*!"

❄

Lenore arrived at the schoolhouse that evening with a joyful heart. Despite everything she had been through the last couple days she had been looking forward to the Christmas program. And now she had even more reason to be happy. She only wished Elijah could be there to see it, but she smiled, certain he'd be able to attend the following year. She looked up towards the ceiling and had a feeling *Grossmammi* was watching from above.

She and Katie put the finishing touches on the stage and made sure all the props were ready while Beth set up the tables for serving cookies, punch and coffee afterwards. The room began to fill with parents and visitors and there was excitement in the air as they mingled before taking their seats.

"Are you nervous?" Katie whispered to Leora.

"*Nee, nee*. The *kinner* have practiced so many times they can practically run the program themselves," she said, giggling. "They'll do wonderful. It'll be the best Christmas program ever... *Gott* is watching over it."

Katie gave her a quick hug. "*Jah*, it will be the best! *Gott* is with us."

Soon it was time for the children to line up at the front of the room and there was a hush in the room. They seemed nervous, but excited at the same time. They took turns reciting poems and singing several songs. Katie clapped loudly as little Anna led many of the songs.

There was a short break as the students dressed in their costumes, and Leora laughed as they rushed about in excitement. The play went perfectly and not one child forgot their lines. The audience clapped for a long moment and looked pleased. She whispered, "*Danke, Gott.*"

There was one final song to the program, and Leora gave a Katie a surprised look as the song ended, and the students immediately led into one more song. She wept tears of joy as she heard them sing a familiar song... *I Surrender All*. Katie gave Leora a knowing smile and nodded. The audience stood to their feet and clapped wildly.

"*Gott, danke, danke*, this *is* the best Christmas program ever!

CHAPTER 10

It was Christmas Day, and the waiting room was filled with Amish people. They all sat with their heads bowed quietly in prayer. Elijah's whole family was there, as well as Tyler and Katie. Leora sat between her two parents; all three of them were still grieving for *Grossmammi*, but the atmosphere in the waiting room was full of hope.

Leora looked up at the clock on the wall. It had been exactly two hours and seven minutes since Elijah had gone into surgery, and the wait was becoming unbearable. The doctors had said it could take as long as three hours for the surgery to be completed.

Her father saw where she was looking and squeezed her hand. "It won't be much longer," he told her. "We must keep praying."

"*Gott* has been so good," Leora said. "I know this is Elijah's miracle."

"I'm so grateful that He used my *mamm*'s death to save a young person." Her mother smiled. "She would have been so happy to see it."

They waited in silence for a few more minutes before Dr. Rivers came in. Everyone jumped to their feet. Dr. Rivers was smiling.

"How did it go?" Hannah asked, clutching her husband's hand.

Dr. Rivers grinned. "I've been waiting seven years to say this," he said. "The transplant surgery went very well. Your son is likely to make a good recovery."

"Praise *Gott!*" cried Hannah. "Thank you, Doctor!" She turned her face into her husband's chest.

"Elijah is still in intensive care, but once he wakes up from the anesthesia, he can have a few visitors," said Dr. Rivers. "Rosie will come to call you when he's awake."

Leora's knees felt weak. She didn't know whether she wanted to cry or sing, but she knew that she was overjoyed. "*Ach, Gott,*" she cried. "*Danke, Gott! Danke!*"

❄

After the Hershbergers had seen Elijah, Leora and her parents were allowed inside. They came in quietly. Elijah looked tired and pale, but he was smiling. There were many more tubes running into his body now, disappearing under the sheet that covered him.

"Elijah." Leora hurried over to him, taking his hand. "How do you feel?"

Elijah smiled at her. "Tired, but okay."

Just then Dr. Rivers walked into the room. "Doctor," he said huskily. "How did it go?"

"It went perfectly, Elijah." Dr. Rivers smiled. "It couldn't have gone any better. You have been given every chance of a full recovery–even a return to normal life."

"Thank you so much." Elijah tried to move and winced a little. "I truly appreciate all you've done."

"Stay still," Dr. Rivers said. "You'll have some pain for a few days, but in two weeks or so, you should be out of hospital. By then your kidney should be doing its job, but you may need more dialysis treatments. If all goes well, then within a year your kidney will be functioning normally." He smiled. "I'll see you a bit later."

Dr. Rivers stepped out of the room. Leora pushed Elijah's hair out of his eyes. "Does it hurt a lot?" she asked.

"*Nee*, not too bad." Elijah looked over to her father. "Peter, I have something to ask you."

"*Jah*?" Leora's father came closer.

"Your *dochtah* is one of the most wonderful people I have ever met," Elijah said. "I have seldom met someone so willing to put others first. And I..." He paused. "I love that. I... love her." He swallowed a little painfully. "I want to ask your permission to court Leora."

There were tears in Peter's eyes. "Elijah, we're honored that Leora's beloved *grossmammi* could save your life," he said. "You are trustworthy and a *gut* man. You may court my *dochtah*."

Elijah looked up at Leora and squeezed her hand. "Would that be all right with you, Leora?" he whispered.

Leora smiled from ear to ear, trembling with joy. "*Jah*," she whispered. "That would be wonderful with me." She looked up at her parents, tears gathering in her eyes. "How great is our *Gott*," she said. "He gives us gifts on His son's birthday. The most wonderful Christmas gifts of all."

Elijah wrapped his arms around her as best as he could, and Leora hugged him back, tears of happiness and sorrow at the same time running down her cheeks. She would miss her *grossmammi* forever, but together, God and *Grossmammi* had given her more than she could ever have asked for.

❆

Two weeks later, Leora waited impatiently outside of the hospital with the Hershbergers' horse and buggy. Even though Ruben and Joshua had volunteered to look after the buggy, she knew better than to leave the two mischievous little boys alone with it. They ran around on the pavement, getting under the horse's legs and shouting.

"Ruben! Joshua!" Leora scolded them. "I hope you're not going to be this noisy around your brother. He's just had an operation, remember?"

"*Jah*, Leora," the boys chorused, and climbed obediently back into the buggy.

Leora laughed and shook her head. Then the glass doors of the hospital opened, and Elijah stepped outside, holding on tightly to his father's arm. Leora beamed, watching him walk slowly out towards her. He was smiling, too. As he reached her, he put his arms around her and gave her a kiss on the forehead. She held him tightly, her heart full of hope and love. "You already feel less bony," she said, with a grin.

"I feel so much better already." Elijah laughed. "The doctors are saying it's a miracle how fast and how well my kidney has already started working. They say that if anyone has a chance of having a normal life on a transplanted kidney, it's me."

"It is a miracle," Leora agreed. "Our Christmas miracle from *Gott*." She smiled up at him, laying a hand on his cheek. "I love you, Elijah."

Elijah grinned. "I love you too. So very much."

Elijah's mother opened the door of the buggy. "Come," she said happily. "Let's go home and celebrate."

"*Jah*," Elijah said. He turned to the buggy and walked slowly towards it, holding Leora's hand. He looked down at her, his eyes dancing. "Let's go celebrate *Gott's* goodness and this wonderful gift from Him."

CHAPTER 11

❄

(Epilogue)

Leora walked slowly through the cemetery. It was summer, and the neatly trimmed grass was a beautiful green. There were some wildflowers growing between the simple gravestones. A soft breeze moved her skirt as she reached a special gravestone and stopped.

"Hello, *Grossmammi*," she said softly. She kneeled down and laid a handful of daisies on the grave. "It's been a while since I've come to visit."

Leora sat down on the grass and gazed out across the green hills. Her heart was filled with a mixture of joy and sadness as she went on. "It has been such a *gut* year and a half since you passed on," she whispered. "So much has happened, but I miss you every single day." A single tear rolled down her cheek. "I wish I could have you hug me one more time, *Grossmammi*. Yet, it was *Gott*'s will for you to go home when you did, and it was part of His plan. I just would have loved for you to see everything that's happened since you went to be with *Gott*."

The only sound she heard in response was the soft cry of a bird in the trees. Leora closed her eyes and felt the warm summer breeze on her face, and her heart was filled with gratitude. "*Gott* has been so *gut* to us," she said. "He always knows best, and I trust His plan no matter how much it hurts."

She sat in silence for a few more moments, allowing gratitude to fill her heart. Then she heard a voice. Turning her head, she saw a figure coming towards her down the hill. She smiled and got up slowly, holding out her arms. "Elijah!"

Elijah strode up to her. His cheeks were red, his eyes shining; he looked healthy and strong. "I thought I would find you here," he said, reaching her.

Leora laid a hand on her stomach. "I had to tell *Grossmammi* the good news that we are going to have a *bobli* of our own," she said. "I know she isn't here in this grave, and perhaps she cannot even hear me, but it feels good to still visit and talk about the things I know she would have wanted to know."

Elijah put his hand over hers, leaned down and kissed her. "Your *Grossmammi* would be so proud of you," he said. "You are a wonderful *frau*, and you are going to be an excellent *mamm* for our *kinner*."

Leora hugged him. "I can't wait to see you as a *daed*," she whispered.

Elijah grinned. "*Jah*, I sure am looking forward to it."

Leora looked up at him, feeling so happy she could burst. "I miss *Grossmammi*, but I'll always be grateful for the last Christmas gift she gave me."

Elijah smiled and gently tucked a loose strand of hair back under her *kapp*. "And what is that?" He asked, his eyes sparkling.

"Your life," she said.

"And we know that all things work together for good to them that love God, to them who are the called according to his purpose." Romans 8:28

The End

If you enjoyed this story and haven't yet read Book 1, *The Christmas Visitor*, you can find it by visiting the link below.
http://www.amazon.com/dp/B07KDTF13P

THANK YOU!

Thank you for reading *A Christmas Miracle*. I hope you were blessed and inspired to see God's faithfulness at work in the lives of the characters. He is always faithful and loves you dearly. Always put your trust in Him! ☺

And one more thing...
If you enjoyed this story, or received inspiration in any way, would you consider leaving a short comment on Amazon with your thoughts? I'd be so very grateful for your support.

Thank you so much!

With love,

Rebekah

MORE BOOKS BY REBEKAH FISHER

Amish Tender Love Box Set- 12-Book Box Set
https://www.amazon.com/dp/B07JQ7115Q

Amish Hearts Collection – 8-Book Box Set
http://www.amazon.com/dp/B07BJHHJRG

www.amazon.com/dp/B078L82FTJ

The Coming Home Series

Tess's Story – Book 1: http://www.amazon.com/dp/B07FMNTTLM
Susan's Story – Book 2: http://www.amazon.com/dp/B07GDQXWR7
Jack's Story – Book 3: http://www.amazon.com/dp/B07H8VM415

A Strange Connection of Hearts Series

Lucy's Story – Book 1: http://www.amazon.com/dp/B0768PWHL1
Martha's Story – Book 2: http://www.amazon.com/dp/B079WGPDKM
Joseph's's Story – Book 3:http://www.amazon.com/dp/B07C329GTW

And more! Check out my author page on Amazon for more titles.
Visit here: www.amazon.com/-/e/B008R715GG

I'd love to have you visit my Facebook page:
http://www.facebook.com/authorrebekahfisher